THE WALES COLLECTION

An anthology of poetry and short stories

Edited by Tim Saunders

Tim Saunders Publications

TS
Tim Saunders Publications

Cover design: Brecon Sky, acrylic by Dawn Harries dawnharriesart.co.uk

As a child, I used to spend nearly all my summer holidays with my aunt in Wales, and we used to catch mackerel in a boat and then cook them on board.

MARY QUANT

CONTENTS

FOREWORD

I am very pleased to introduce this anthology of stories and poetry from Wales-based writers, including those inspired by Wales, with its rich cultural heritage, historic castles and tradition of myths and legends.

It was in my early twenties that I first briefly visited Wales, driving with my companion to Holyhead to catch the ferry to Ireland. I remember stopping off en route and feeling awe-inspired by the majestic mountains in the distance. I turned to my companion and remarked, "I'd love to live here one day."

I did not return to Wales until two decades later when I visited Anglesey on the advice of a work colleague. Knowing nothing about the area, I opened a map on my computer, closed my eyes and placed my finger on the screen. I hit upon a little town called Benllech. A friend and I were soon on the train from London, excited to visit this new world. As we eventually approached the North Wales coastline, I had the unexpected and emotion-provoking sense of coming home.

Returning to North Wales numerous times on

holiday I explored the surroundings like an excited child; strolling along the expanses of beach and visiting medieval buildings such as the castles in Beaumaris and Conwy and the 12th century monastery at Penmon. Then, seven years after that initial trip to Anglesey, I settled into my house in Benllech. A few days later, I was invited to join Copper Writers, a group based in Brynteg, with sessions held in the atmospheric, vaulted-ceilinged room of a converted chapel. I felt at home there, too. With a fellow writer, I began to explore the beautiful sites of Anglesey, including Red Wharf Bay and Bull Bay, and the village of Moelfre, which is steeped in maritime history and affords incredible sea views from the Lifeboat Station. The rugged beauty of the South Stack is another source of breathtaking vistas and for me reminiscent of my cherished Land's End in Cornwall.

Cemaes is a charming village on the north coast of Anglesey, sited on Cemaes Bay. Fellow Copper Writers and I were delighted to recite poetry in the village hall on St David's Day. I chose the work of Dylan Thomas after reintroducing myself to his poetry while researching Welsh culture. I also partook of visits to local galleries, including the Oriel Mon in Llangefni, therein discovering the works of Welsh artists such as Kyffin Williams and Gwilym Pritchard.

My hankering for green spaces has been satisfied by trips to the stunning Newborough Forest and Nature Reserve and I still have the opportunity for extensive exploration of ancient sites such as burial chambers and stone circles. But over and above all of this I have the great fortune of enjoying the wonders of Anglesey from my own home. Each and every day, soon after waking, I open my blinds and gaze at the mountains on one side and the expanse of Irish sea on the other and I still cannot quite believe that I am resident in this spiritual land. The Isle of Anglesey continues to enrich my poetry and to provide a haven away from the maelstrom of city life, which can instil a weariness in the psyche. Half a century spent between Glasgow and London had taken their toll, and I never cease to be overwhelmed with an extraordinary sense of relief at having found such a haven of peace.

The therapeutic lappings of the waves on Benllech Beach instil a kind of magic in the soul that can only serve to hasten the flow of creativity and it is unsurprising that other areas of Wales would facilitate the flutterings of the muse.

This book, with its eclectic writings, will surely provide something for every reader and provide a chance to transcend the everyday and I thoroughly recommend it to you.

Mary Cochrane

POETRY

THE OWL AND THE PUSSY CAT IN CARDIFF BAY

The owl and the pussycat went to sea
I was invited to do the commentary.
Owl strummed his guitar to a serenade in
a beautiful boat, a pea green shade
the cat looked up at the shining stars
distracted by restaurants and coffee bars
they took Manuka honey on wholemeal bread
declaring to me they'd like to get wed
they took plenty of money wrapped
in a five-pound note
inflation meant, it didn't cover hire of the boat
they sailed away around Cardiff Bay to the land
where bong trees grew
the bong trees were replaced by luxury
flats, a sign of all things new.
They spotted a pig, not at the edge of a wood,
but by the entrance of Techniquest
"Dear piggy are you willing to sell for one
shilling your ring?" was the owls request.
He declined one shilling but for
twenty pounds he sold
his nose ring, assayed at nine carat gold
the cat and the owl left me in the lurch

and decided to wed in the Norwegian Church.
They needed a turkey, one was found
outside the Senedd walking around
the elegant fowl, feathers sprayed with gel
booked their wedding reception at St David's Hotel.
They dined on mince and slices of quince,
ate with a Welsh, love spoon
with paw in claw at the edge of the shore,
they danced by the light of the moon.
The rhythm was of 'strictly' class as they
waltzed around the Roald Dahl Plass.

Lorraine Gray

THE CARDIFF HALF MARATHON

Thirteen miles runners expect to do
starting from Lloyd George Avenue.
A sea of people flow from Cardiff Bay
colourful, snakelike, on their way.
Fifteen thousand bodies determined to run
serious, passionate or having fun.
Sweating blue Smurfs scurry by
their weeks of training justify.
Batman without Robin, clowns with balloons
listening on iPods to time passing tunes.
Raffia skirted men, two little chicks
someone dragging a long crucifix.
Pounding along for each deserving cause
crowds encourage with cheers and applause
Cancer, Parkinson's Noah's Ark Appeal
money for research or helping to heal.
Different sizes fast and slow
fit and unfit - ready steady go.
Two joggers carrying Thomas the Tank
generous people the charities will thank.
Blistered feet, muscles cramped and sore
forget the pain - a few miles more.
Checking their watches, sipping water

hoping their best time is slightly shorter
spectators feel complete admiration
wishing they had athletic dedication.
Every runner achieving an internal reward
and each of them we sincerely applaud.

Lorraine Gray

CLARK'S PIES

If you visit Grangetown, a must for you to try
oval shaped, lightly browned, famous Clark's pie.
Full of meat and gravy, a mouth-watering delight
just the very thought of it will whet your appetite.
Mary Clark the founder devised this recipe
frequently enjoyed, for dinner, lunch, or tea.
Pastry melts in your mouth; gravy rich and brown
a pint of Brains Dark can help wash it down.
Never share a Clarksies pie, eat it piping hot
nibble around the edges, ensure you scoff the lot!
After paying for your pie, never ever wait
consume it immediately, don't put it on a plate.
Don't spoil the taste with sauce,
dismiss brown or red
forget the knife and fork, use your hands instead.
Cardiff City players insist upon their treat
Bluebirds always need protein from the meat.
Ignore calories, grams of fat; you don't need to know
remember these pies were invented a century ago.
At Bromsgrove Street corner smell before you buy
a tasty traditional scrumptious Clarksies pie.

Lorraine Gray

THE CARDIFF CASTLE ANIMAL WALL

When I was young and very small
I ran in fear past the animal wall.
Fifteen creatures to pounce on me
their threatening features I could see.
My grandmother, when as a little child
like me, thought the wall was wild.
But through the decades these stony creatures
have been one of Cardiff's cherished features.

The conception was in 1866
an animal wall of old stone bricks.
William Burgess' drafted design
for the Marquis of Bute, third in line.
After Burgess' death assistant
brought to completion the wall of fame.

Thomas Nicholls sculpted nine beasts in all
and by 1890 were perched on the wall.
Their naturalistic paint soon weathered
away exposing stonework as seen today.

Castle Street was widened in 1922
as the volume of traffic constantly grew

the wall still standing good and strong
after being moved fifty metres along.

The creatures when you scrutinise
stare back at you with glassy eyes
bear, lioness, wolf, apes and seal
lions, hyena - have scare appeal.

Six further sculptures made in 1931
by Alexander Carrick, creatively done.
Anteater, leopard and scavenger vulture
were added to this iconic structure.
Finally the pelican and the masked raccoon
looking eerie under the midnight moon.

In 2010 this wall was refaced
the anteater had his nose replaced.
Restoration and cleaning eyes of glass
admired by tourists as they pass.

On the animal wall surprises were seen
during the Roald Dahl centenary 2016.
Rabbit, panda, and owl weren't expected
but appeared in the city of the unexpected.

Welsh rugby fans belt out Celtic sounds
echoing over the wall to the castle grounds.
Listening through time this menagerie clan
have heard Men of Harlech and Calon Lân.

Cut from sandstone these animal carvings

have watched BMX bikes and penny farthings.
T Ford cars chauffeuring Victorian ladies
and scantily clad women in fast Mercedes.

Lorraine Gray

LANDMARKS/ SCULPTURES - CARDIFF BAY

From Tiger Bay to Cardiff Bay old and new
sculptures and landmarks, to name a few.

Near the Millennium Centre, stands a literate fellow
a bronze/granite sculpture of Ivor Novello
actor, composer with songs and tales
born, 1893 in Cardiff, Wales.

By the Norwegian Church a monumental sight
made from mosaic in icy white.
Captain Robert Scott's non-returnable trip

sailed from Cardiff on the Terra Nova Ship.

Wife on an Ocean Wave appealing and fun
in a tin bath they sit with their small son.
The boy catching fish or at least doing his best
this work is situated near Techniquest.

Outside the Senedd a memorial in black
represents merchant seamen who never came back.
A combined head and hull on the seabed lay
where wreathes are placed on Poppy Day.

Looking across the Barrage through wind, and rain
stands a young couple with their Great Dane.
Namely People Like Us photographed each day
are typical characters, from the old Tiger Bay.
Hess carrying a newspaper wearing dungarees
she's holding her shoe, exposing her knees.

Fronting the Pier Head building greatly admired
are four red/black cannons - silent - unfired.

At Britannia Quay in cast bronze steel
a Miner stands against a pit winding wheel.
Pick axe in hand, perhaps spare a thought
the name behind it Pit to Port.

Those Beastie Benches are favourites of mine
red brick built in Roald Dahl's design.

This spiritual figure overlooks Cardiff Bay

representing peace and harmony every day.
World Peace Dreamer, aptly named
holding the peace torch brightly enflamed.

Towards the wetlands seagulls fly in a flock
the Rope Knot a reminder of where
ships would dock.

Lorraine Gray

DAFFODILS

Early March they start to bloom
perfume drifts throughout my room.
Scattered groups on grass of green
Celtic flowers in abundance seen.
Daffodils in bright display
inspiring William one April day -
back in the year 1804
he wrote of treasures we adore.

A magnitude of golden bliss
gentle as a lover's kiss.
Roath Park Lake and River Taff
accommodate the dancing daff.
The sun, moon and star filled sky
watch these flowers multiply.
In pensive mood I fix my stare
his poetic vision I long to share.

The fluttering dancers of the spring
make my heart with pleasure sing.
I observed this happy vibrant crowd
as I wandered lonely as a cloud.

Lorraine Gray

Lorraine Gray was born in Cardiff and has lived in Cardiff Bay for 27 years. She is married to Terry and has three children, four grandchildren and one great grandson. A retired fitness instructor she still keeps fit by weight training, playing table tennis and walking many miles usually around the Bay where she gets inspiration for her writing, which she finds very therapeutic. She has written many poems and short stories. Lorraine belongs to U3A writing group in Cardiff and she says that attending a class keeps her motivated.

HIRAETH

There's a word in the Welsh language
that means homesickness.
A longing for a place that you can never return to.
A place that no longer exists.
Hiraeth.

Ten lanterns burned bright that night, each
containing a wish, a hope, a dream.
Ten golden spheres.
You sang the Billy Joel song at the top of your voice
a war dance into the new decade.

Red hair like campfire flames
dazzling bright
shining in the dark night.
Bare feet stamp on cold earth.

We lit our lanterns and shut our eyes
the air smelt cold, of smoke.
We thought of our wishes, set them
free and watched them soar
gold on black.

How was I to know that we would
become our lanterns?

Some stuck in trees, held onto by sharp branches
some soared high into the sky,
away from the others.

Some never left the ground, their
flame extinguished too soon.
Too early.

How was I to know that would be our last night?

The last night we danced?
The last night we laughed?
The last night we sang?

Hiraeth, I think upon the word,
it covers me like an old blanket.

Hiraeth

I can never return yet I reside there forever.

Julie Barnett

Julie Barnett is a writer from Swansea. Winner of The British Theatre Challenge 2019, winner of Pint Sized Plays international playwriting competition, nominated for the Anne Bartram Playwright Award, shortlisted for Chippy Lane New Writers Award. Julie's plays have been performed nationally and internationally. Julie is enjoying the new challenge of writing spoken word poetry and has had poems performed by Anthroplay Theatre and SlaMinutes at The Pleasance Theatre, London. Julie lives in Pontarddulais with her husband and two small boys.

CONSTITUENCY OF BRECON AND RADNORSHIRE

Election Day, May 2010

The flattened sandstone peaks of Pen y Fan farewell
their springtime snows. I place my democratic cross
beside one name amongst the nameless. None may
tell whom I elect nor consequential gain or loss.
Beyond the streams of Fforest Fawr the soldiers play
at death, with loaded arms and inimitable might.
Though civil settlements collapse, claims pass
away, we may not be disorderly, we must not fight.
A kestrel hovers over Twyn y Gaer. We shout
aloud at that we have achieved: we
breathe, we bless, we freely speak (albeit
limited in that we speak about),
we acquiesce - above all else, we acquiesce.
So should I stroll up Llyn y Plyfin? There's
the rub: we may select our entertainment,
health care, shoes, the bits and pieces
of our lives - all but the hub,
the core: in voting we deny our right to choose.

Mike Douse

BURIED TRUTHS

There is significance in falling snow,
meanings in how it slants across the field
and clutters up my spectacles.
How sheep, heavy with sock and
scarf, appear to know
what each may share must to the shearer yield,
with every drift perfidious and deep.
The Beacons lie before the ewes, yet still
the shepherd and his crook may fleece their flock,
much as the two-faced flake precipitates
the springtime grass on every sunlit hill,
yet dissipates as winter's aftershock
seasons the lambs before their sell-by dates:
and I would tell the world what that implies
were sonnets more than fourteen lines in size.

Mike Douse

CARDIFF REFLECTION

As I strolled into Queen's Arcade I saw
this lout with dreadful mien,
bedraggled arrogance displayed,
crude as a drunk at Hallowe'en.

You foul unshaven, lurching yob
how dare you spoil my ambling thus,
you unkempt thug, you hirsute slob,
why can't you be the same as us?

Straight at my path this ruffian strode
unmindful of my being there
my space, my route, my rights, my road:
he lumbered onward without care.

So taken was I by his gall
I tripped in dazed catastrophe
and almost shattered in my fall
the mirror that confronted me...

Mike Douse

LLYN Y FAN FACH

Crisp crystalline the glacial day, wild
winnowing the storm.
Emerging from the eel-grey lake,
across the sandstone shore
she comes, as from another time,
age-old in lissom form
but to these waters must return and
grace my hills no more.
Once, twice now thrice the proffered
poisoned implements
touch too metallically her truth-white
arm. As if in pain she cries. I hear her
still. My poignant sentiments
of bitter love drove her away. She
shall not come again.
Oh wretched, deporting iron. I gladly would forsake
my farm, my anvil and my horse:
its bridle and my plough
for just a shadowed movement deep
in Little Fan's cold lake.
Wild Wales of myths and megaliths:
would I might sooth her now.

Mike Douse

Mike Douse has worked in education internationally since 1963. His publications include An Enjoyment of Education, One World One School, and numerous (and readily-accessible online) journal articles and conference presentations, along with three collections of his poems: Old Ground, Gone to Ground, and Grounded. He is living happily ever after in Mountain Ash, Rhondda Cynon Taf, with his dear wife Patricia.

LOW ABOVE THE TREES

Wait at this Welsh lakeside at dusk
and you will hear, faint at first,
the ancient, haunting cries of geese;
hear and suddenly see them,
fast and low above the trees.
They bank and glide and slice the lake,
defacing its mirror; disappear briefly
in pink, parallel showers of spray.

Their cries are not for us,
nor for anything they can see.
Their message is not personal;
it simply states the law:
of the stuff of stars which must be shared,
bequeathed, so the message can live as long
as the atoms of its words.
We are free to linger and listen;
it does not matter
if we grasp what we hear.

Come again to the water at daybreak
and see untucking heads, uncoiling necks,
an unfolding and stretching of wings.
The geese honk softly each to each
of the strenuous, necessary business

of taking to the air; the advantages
of slip-streaming, of getting airborne together.
And having settled that, they leave
across the lake a formation of stripes,
diminishing wakes, wingtip splashes:
ripples which subside to nothing,
to a mirror.

Alan Hawley

ON A HILL BY A RIVER

I am
the stumps of a castle
on a hill by a river.

I have lived
four lives of oaks;
half the time since the Romans left.

I speak
Norman French, Middle English, Welsh,
cell-phone vernacular.

I dream
sometimes,
of the next real Prince of Wales.

My name:
Newtown calls me
Old Town.

What can I tell you?
The Daily Mail notwithstanding,
the climate really is changing.

What do I fear?

Not much. Perhaps that I might one day
not sleep again under turf and trees.

What would I have you do?
You could get rid of these railings:
they're a bit itchy.

Alan Hawley

 Born in London E17 Alan was educated near but not at Harrow School. He survived an explosives course, that is, a chemistry degree, at Bristol University and got a stop-gap job as a civil servant, which lasted until retirement. In between, Alan got married, an Arabian horse, in that order, and then another Arabian horse and so on. They moved to Wales, to a demolishable house with nice stables and fields. "We really like it here," he says. He came across a Lifetime Learning leaflet, which mentioned creative writing. "Writing is just words, and I know plenty. Easy. Or so I thought," he says...

ANGLESEY

Isle of Anglesey, Ynys Mon,
Mam Cymru – land of wheat and corn.
Before the time men call the dawn,
from fire and water were you born?

Rock-strewn, sandy beaches fair,
shy lair of seals and seabirds rare.
The feet of saints have trodden there,
breathing your salt-encrusted air.

There's a presence, sometimes felt
in secret groves where Druids dwelt,
where penitents and preachers knelt –
the secret of that island Celt.

Sheep in woollen winter rags
shelter beneath rude slate-hewn flags,
munching marsh-grass, stump tails a-wag,
across the Straits from Snowdon's crags.

Flower-flecked field to mossy marsh
the ancients of this land still pass.
And ghosts of Roman legions march
across the short, sheep-nibbled grass.

Kings and Princes came and went.
An arrogant Julius Caesar sent
the might of Rome, his captains bent
on conquest – mon recalcitrant.

Sun-scorched, wind scoured to the bone,
a monolith that stands alone.
Once crafted from pre-Cambrian stone,
this sea-washed island I call home.

Kay Middlemiss

CHURCH ISLAND

*Church Island is an island graveyard in the
Menai Strait. Situated between the Britannia
and Menai Bridges, it is reached by a causeway
from the Anglesey shoreline. Saint Tysilio's
church was founded in the sixth century.*

Wrapped in morning's grey, streaked red,
cold, silent island of the dead.
Row on row, those who have been
but are no more – those unseen.
Between the bridges' loud embrace
sea birds and traffic's musical solace.
They lie.
Lie gazing sightless at the sky.
Dressed in their best
boots, suits or dress.
The rich, the poor, humble or proud,
in a cloud of gauze or a winding shroud.
The wise, the loud,
the humble, the cowed.
They lie.
Lie wrapped in sleep as I pass by.
In a sleep from which there is no waking,
no tomorrow, no new day breaking.
Dawns will come and evenings go

in a haze of heat or cold, white snow.
But not for you beneath these stones
in a tumble of grumbling, crumbling bones.
You wait.
Wait for the keeper of the gate.
'til the trumpets cry,
and the oceans sigh,
then your soul will fly away.
First to ashes, then to dust,
as all things, eventually, must.

Kay Middlemiss

Following a career in the airline industry where she was fortunate to see the world, mixing with many nationalities and cultures, Kay moved to the beautiful Isle of Anglesey. "We renovated a near-derelict converted church with a large garden, dogs, cats and flock of pigeons: inspirations for many stories," she says. "With Joy Mawby — also represented in this book — we formed Copper Writers." The group has published two anthologies of work by local writers and part-organized the first Anglesey Writing Festival. Kay writes for pleasure, not profit, enjoying competitions and writing events.

THE BITTERNS ARE BOOMING TONIGHT

I came here to be alone, to revel in my one-ness,
to reflect, and search for solace, to
find the song in my soul.
The tune's been off-key for a while, the
beat of my heart out of kilter.
The breeze shivers the reeds like waves
and whispers its passing sigh.
I know I'm not by myself
by the nearby ruffles and scuffles. The call of the
curlew chills me, matching my melancholy mood.
Grey clouds shift — edges turning yellow,
catching from somewhere the evening
sun, and then I hear, from deep in the
marsh, the booming of the bitterns.
I listen to the tuneless refrain; transfixed,
my heartbeat responds.
Filled with the peace of Anglesey's marshland
I turn towards home re-tuned because —
the bitterns are booming tonight.

Edwina Jones

Edwina lives on Ynys Môn and is Welsh-speaking

 but she mainly writes in English. She has just finished her first novel and also writes short stories and poetry. She belongs to two writing groups. She was secretary for the Môntage committee, which produced two anthologies of work from local authors and was also involved in organising a writing festival on the island.

DO NOT CALL IT WINTERTIME ON ANGLESEY

Do not call it wintertime on Anglesey.
Think only of today with the nut-sweet smell
of leaves which crunch underfoot.
A parliament of rooks and a few remaining
leaves clot the black branches of the sycamore
against an angry sky.

Think only of today
when the church stands dark and
stark in frosty fields.
Lino print on a silver backdrop.

Do not call it wintertime
when the wind whips salty white waves higher
than a lighthouse and the spray has rainbows in it.

Think only of today
when mist rises from the marsh,
half-shrouding a chapel's ruins.
Film-set for a melodrama.

Do not call it wintertime

when a slit of crimson brilliance pierces
the slate-grey morning sky at sunrise.
God's letterbox, the children call it.

Think only of today
when bracken glows bronze and gold and the
world is upside down in the calm, clear lake.

Do not call it wintertime
for the garden proudly shows a vagrant rose,
nasturtiums, and chrysanthemums.
There's a vivid goldfinch on the bird table,
a red squirrel shares the seed.
He leaps, spreadeagles on our neighbour's
wall and, spider-like scampers — flaming
copper on new-washed pebbledash.

So, go on, say, "It's wintertime on Anglesey."
Think of today, when, with summer's
lush abundance gone,
we have the time and space to see this winter's
jewels and treasure them. While, in the dark,
below the ground, a harvest waits for spring.

Joy Mawby

Joy lives on the Isle of Anglesey in North Wales.
She runs a local writing group and was involved
in the production of two anthologies of work, by
Anglesey writers and in organising the first Writing
Festival to be held on the island. She has written and

published three memoirs of other peoples' lives and her own memoir – although this is specially for her grandchildren. Two of her plays have been staged locally and she also writes short stories and poetry.

OTTERS AT THE GANN

Sky loaned her softness
whispered her warmth
on marram grass,
reflected her colours;
rivulets below
flow slowly through
this salty marsh.

Sustained silence,
stillness serene,
this unspoiled space
asleep between
sky and sea
creatures free
they captivate.

Ripples on water,
dark shadow shows,
disappears 'til
an arrow grows,
glistens and glows
shows us where
this quiet one goes.

More water dances,

sun's jewels erupt
pups in pursuit
swim smoothly
they tease the eye
hold focus fast
freeze this moment...

'A time of rapture
captured in the mind
lasts for ever.'

Stillness held fast
a robin aloft a sloe's branch
contributed.

Dinnella Shelton

 Born and bred in the Rhymney
Valley, Dinnella deserted to Devon
to train as a teacher. Now retired
she enjoys a dual existence. Her
roots and main home are still in
that same valley. Her heart and
happy place are lodged firmly in Pembrokeshire.
Her love affair with its coast and hills continues to
grow. "I can read, write, paint, walk and talk with
absolute freedom amidst it's stunning scenery and
lovely people. I want my poetry to reflect this," says
Dinnella, who belongs to Bedwas Writers' Circle.

PEAT MEN

Cors Caron

They rise from the marsh, bog-smeared,
stinking of ale and a thousand years of peat.

Under the right moon, you'll see them
cut-and-come-again, dark burdens shouldering

the night, tongues slackened by loosestrife.
A place of wings and water, holding its ghosts

beneath spikes of asphodel and bedstraw,
a hustle of bees in rosebay, where cotton-grass

is buffeted to tufts of ribboned fleece,
and stars of butterwort fold gently over flesh.

Their sword was a spade, anger a red-hot spark
kindled each day inside a simple croft;

dirt covering the raw wound of their poverty,
the blistered hands that laboured long and hard

for this sullen-burning harvest. Men who sang
of ash, and lodged their hearts in earth,

dug futures from the mire, where one day
they'd be buried, pleached to roots of alder.

Kathy Miles

Originally from Liverpool, Kathy
Miles is a poet and short story
writer living in West Wales. Her
work has appeared widely in
magazines and anthologies, and
her fourth full collection of poetry,
Bone House, was published by Indigo Dreams in
2020. Kathy is a previous winner of the Bridport
Prize, as well as the Welsh Poetry and Wells
Literature Festival Competitions, and the 2022
Shepton Mallet Snowdrop Competition. She has an
MA in Creative Writing from the University of Wales
Trinity Saint David and is a regular book reviewer
and workshop facilitator.

AFFLICTED

I love you in the daytime,
when the wind howls through
my treasured home in Ynys Mön.
I love you as I gaze upon the turbulent sea;
your lovely face freeze-framed
in the midst of that mercurial reverie.

I love you in the black of night,
when the world is asleep
and my aching bones, not old but
weary beyond their years,
impress upon me
the ephemeral nature of all things.

I am taken back to the beginning:
the small, naked boy in the kitchen sink,
shivering and baffled by the weekly ritual.
My heart simultaneously bursts with joy and pain,
and in that moment I am not so afflicted by
your death.I love you in the daytime,
when the wind howls through
my treasured home in Ynys Môn.
I love you as I gaze upon
the turbulent sea;
your lovely face freeze-framed

in the midst of that mercurial reverie.
I love you in the black of night,
when the world is asleep
and my aching bones, not old
but weary beyond their years,
impress upon me the ephemeral
nature of all things.
I am taken back to the beginning:
the small, naked boy in the kitchen sink,
shivering and baffled by the weekly ritual.
My heart simultaneously bursts with
joy and pain,
and in that moment I am not so
afflicted by your death.

Mary Cochrane

THE WAVES

Wednesday, May 8, 2019
Mary and her six friends from Copper Writers
visit the Lifeboat Station in Moelfre:

Take shelter from the wild winds
and driving rain;
read of horrors at sea:
mariners and travellers in distress;
submarine sinking;
shipwreck of the Royal Charter
with its pots of rare gold;
stories of bravery, heroics, determination;
the willingness to risk life to save
the lives of others,
and yet:
the sense of calm wrought by the
incredible vistas and
the waves:
today crashing in, furiously, wildly
beautiful, mesmerising.
We brave the elements to visit
the statue of Dic Evans.
The wind threatens to dislodge me
from the steps
and toss me into the turbulent sea.
The waves:

the sound of Heaven
in a world otherwise crumbling.
The waves:
violent, hurling themselves up
the steep bank and onto the steps.
The waves:
rushing into my very soul.
I am alone, breathless, complete.

Mary Cochrane

THE WILDEST OF UNKNOWN PLACES

I want to see that Copper Mountain
or walk in corridors of ancient castles
built by warring kings.
I want to run on sandy beaches
where vast expanses of sea
gently convey their history.
Another trip to Bull Bay or Red Wharf.

Or the rugged terrain of the South Stack.
Take me back so that I can fill my lungs
with that pure Anglesey air
and feel one last surge of heroism
in my wilting form.
The piper is calling;
the roar is pounding in my head.
Place all your hopes in me
as I go intrepid into
the wildest of unknown places.

Mary Cochrane

WHO I AM

Clippity-clop, the world has stopped,
for logical reason or fate,
I dream of that Gothic seascape
hanging over the fireplace,
and my own virtuoso performance
on the piano;
seated in my red velvet gown,
with the sound of miracles encroaching
upon the gloom.
Come now to my silent rooms
and speak to me in hushed Celtic tones
that signify a rare form of significance.
Let me unravel in the Cymrian rain
and finally remember who I am.

Mary Cochrane

THE MAGIC OF YNYS MÔN

I'm home at last,
in the place where dreams ride
on the wanton sea,
and elegant ladies gaze
through stained-glass windows
at their flowering shrubbery.
The piece from Rigoletto
playing on the piano
in the sunlit room
flows from my own hands,
as I hear the distant voice
of the rugged Welsh man.
And how still the night!
When my soul laments
but still spurs me on;
attuned to the magic
of Ynys Môn.

Mary Cochrane

PASSING THROUGH

Welsh mountains, firmly within my view;
fresh, snow-capped, permanent.
I'm passing through;
a temporary marker in your life,
and gladly fading;
the soil, neatly parted and waiting
like a lifeless womb.
Just one last surge of memories;
a heyday, a glorious dream,
then the finale,
BLACK.

Mary Cochrane

NO ADVANCE AND
NO RETREAT

A swish of leaves on a September day
evoked a sense of immediacy;
time adrift and waiting to be filled,
vast arenas of potential stilled.
Shadows take shape and vie for precedence
in a mind intent on recklessness.
The mirror image, hopeless to deny
cruelty that alludes to days gone by:
days gone by, played out in a parody
of a present life marred by malady;
a set of repetitive entities
violating with obscenities.
And the crucial question, not subdued,
affronts the mind with great discord:
with no advance and no retreat
how can the past and future meet?

Mary Cochrane

SUICIDALITY

He lived in the back streets,
with the smell of whisky and hashish
suspended in the sullen air
of solitude and wasted dreams.
Smithereens of a broken personality
lay like invisible ruins
in the rooms of his run-down flats
in the mean parts of Britain's cities.
Left in the back streets,
falling into a dark place of no return;
blood-stained emptiness
and the shattered lives left behind,
screaming into a world that didn't listen.
SUICIDALITY -
just another symptom of modern living.

Mary Cochrane

THE SWAY OF THE NIGHTINGALE'S SONG

In the sway of the nightingale's song
I will dance with the stars above,
and depart from my sweet Ynys Môn
when the world is abundant with love.
I will dance with the stars above
when your soul is attuned to my own.
When the world is abundant with love,
I'll be beckoning you back home.
As your soul is attuned to my own,
in a flourish of ecstasy,
I'll be beckoning you back home
to a sense of belonging with me.
In a flourish of ecstasy
we will run with our wraiths and our kin.
With a sense of belonging we'll be
awakened to Heaven again.
We will run with our wraiths and our kin
and depart from my sweet Ynys Môn;
awakened to Heaven again,
in the sway of the nightingale's song.

Mary Cochrane

BRIGHT RAYS OF TRUTH

Mystical Aurora, flashing green,
dancing spirits on a sky-screen;
beyond the limits of fragile Earth,
borne of the sun's omnipotent breadth.
Red star burning for eternity,
till I am you and you are me;
merged with the deep, and companionless;
no life or death as our honoured guest.
And the shipwreck lies with faded blooms,
in the world below, in the lonely rooms
where wraiths and poets engage in vain thoughts
of bright rays of truth that cannot be sought.

Mary Cochrane

INCONSEQUENTIAL LIVING

You need to come home to me -
to bring that sweet sense
of the earth shifting.
I need to see those eyes
that shame the stars
and convey their yearnings
without a single word.
I want to be your lover
before the treacherous breath of time
withers me as it withers all.
One moment in that tornado-like rush
and I will forego a decade
of inconsequential living.

Mary Cochrane

 Mary Cochrane was born in Glasgow to Irish-immigrant parents and began to write poetry at the age of seven. She moved to London at the age of twenty-one where she studied psychology at Goldsmiths College, attaining a BSc (Hons) and PhD.

Her career at the Institute of Psychiatry ended after a battle with cancer and subsequent ill-health. It was then that she resumed with her creative writing and has now self-published six books of poetry. In 2017 Mary moved to Anglesey where she spends her time writing and painting, inspired by the beauty of the island.

THE HANGING OF DIC PENDERYN

Poem for Richard Lewis aka Dic Penderyn executed for a crime he did not commit on August 13, 1831.

Have you heard, have you heard?
They are hanging Dic Penderyn again.
They are hanging him in Moscow
and New York state.
They are hanging him in London
from the Traitors' Gate.

They are hanging him in Britain
and many foreign lands.
They are hanging him in cities
and upon the desert sands.
Dic Penderyn has had many names
throughout the whole wide world;
Albert Parsons, Blair Peach, Carlo Giuliani
and countless others you've never heard,
who will live forever in the hearts of the many.

They could not kill him in Cardiff,
London, Kent State or Illinois
for that man of Merthyr

Dic Penderyn he shall never die.
When people fight oppression
we know who leads the way.
That's why we say
long Live Dic Penderyn
Yesterday, tomorrow and today.

Phil Knight

BONES

Down, down below sound
under a man made sea
the drowned church bells
ring out cold calling to me.
The choir of bones
sings on in the still waters
and the red tide
plays a tune on the hill.
The names of the fallen
are not to be read
on any day of honour
for the living or the dead.
Washed are the streets
forgotten under time.
The weight of water
is greater than stone or lime.
A purple palimpsest,
this reservoir bruise remains,
a reminder of an impotent people.
Welsh protests down English drains.

Phil Knight

TRUNKS

Gnoll Park, Neath

Beyond the Memorial Gates
and their stone testaments,
a Tarmac road divides
an arcade of imperial trees.
Some are left wild,
others have been amputated
by the parks department.
Bare of branches
these totem trunks stand
like Corinthian columns
of a collapsed temple.
A hundred yards in
and traffic static ends
and a sort of silence reigns.

Phil Knight

 Phil Knight is a poet from Neath in South Wales. He has been published in Red Poets, Earth love, Poetry Wales, Atlantic Review and other publications. In 2015 Red Poets published his poetry collection You Are Welcome To Wales.

WHEN IT'S LOVE BUT IT'S NOT LOVE

It's hard telling the difference between the two.
They are identical twins both born
from the same womb.
Breastfed by the same mother
taught by the same dad
they both had a likeness; neither good nor bad.
Together they were, through day and through night
no trouble they caused; they were raised quite right.
They were identical twins
in conjunction they belonged.
Telling them apart was unnecessary
so where did it all go wrong?
This part is blurry.
Was it day, was it night?
Perhaps there was rain or maybe
the sun shone bright.
Nonetheless
the change was transparent
we could see it all crystal clear
through the feelings of rapid heart beats
nerves laughing,
blushing, and tears.
Love became irrational

full of both heartbreaks and shame
love became selfish, ruining its own name.
love remained simple through
day and through night
no trouble, love caused; love was raised quite right.

Amberina Larg

Before moving to Wales to pursue her dream of becoming a writer, Amberina lived on the island of Brunei where she starred as Moana in Musical Mania. "I love to create stories from my dreams and objects in front of me," she says. Amberina took part in a reality show called Got what it takes, commissioned by CBBC.

A UKRAINIAN
WOMAN DREAMS
(of a garden of peace)

Above the bombs hiss like snakes,
she gathers her headscarf
into a trellis for the doves
and flowers of her thoughts.

She walks the path,
with heavy headed petals in their sleep,
not quite believing the hues of slumber,
or bold courage of the sunflower,
its gold sheen
tracing new paths in her hand.

Until the doors of darkness
open out to the cornfields
that run together in one yellow river.

And the shadows of her mind
desire to dive in
and turn into something golden.

Jacqueline Jones

THE KEYHOLE

The shock left
a shuddering comet tail.

The day had come
that she could not even
read her name.

In fever no. 19
that rose from the desert.

Hieronymus Bosch
glimpsed through the keyhole.
Medicine men applying treatments
and moulding features,
the ground had eyes.

She wanted to scream,
nurses told her
the bars were just virtual reality.

She raised her voice
and they shattered.

Jacqueline Jones

THREE CLIFFS BAY

We scrambled down cliffs like young goats
answering the call of cresting waves
laughing, running against the wind.

Youth so precious, captured like
footprints in shifting sand,
the strength of the sea carried us on
undulating, rippling up and down.

We ran back shaking wet like puppies
the languor of love seeped through
as sun warmed our unblemished skin.

A day of memories...
love, youth, freedom
under the secrecy of a Welsh sky.

Valerie Ingram

Valerie was born in Cardiff and she is widowed with two children. "I never knew where the desire to write poetry came from until, after an exhausting day with my two year old, I sat down to write to relieve the stress," she recalls. "This led to my mother telling me that my Danish father had also been a poet. My eldest child started in junior school, like me, to write poetry but it was called lyrics for music. Is poetry in my blood? I hope so, and that it flows in the generations to come."

Valerie belongs to Bedwas Writing Group.

WHAT IF...

What if that wonderful wild Orangutan
of distant Borneo
being chased along the trunk of a felled forest tree
by man's extension – a JCB...
What if he leapt in the air with superhuman ability
to land in the cab of his human
aggressor and throttle him
and turn the machine
on the other trucks to smash them?
And what if he sent a screech of
suprahuman audibility
that called back his brothers and
sisters fleeing from the forest
to join him in his attack?
And
what if a young activist from Rainforest Rescue
shared a video of this event across the world
which caused all pension funds to sell their holdings
in companies associated with deforestation
for palm oil or soy bean plantations
or cattle ranches or habitations?
What if we stopped exploiting the earth
and started to share it with all wild fauna and flora?

Angie Gliddon

Angie was a biologist working in medical research. While bringing up her two children she grew fruit and veg. When she retired, Angie looked forward to writing for fun. When she joined the Copper Writers Group on Anglesey, Angie enjoyed their supportive environment and was involved in preparing the first two Anglesey Writing Festivals. Her hobbies include natural history and rambling when the paths are not steep! She once was a political activist but now has no confidence in most leaders, who don't recognise the threat of climate change to our world.

CROESO I GYMRU*

It is a land of coastlines, turreted
castles, misty mountain tops.
Awesome scenery, woolly sheep,
bleating in their flocks.
Land of song floats over,
the terrain's craggy rocks.

As I travel along the bridge,
with trepidation, I cross.
Only to meet homely, humble abodes
of white cottages, I see.

At the Gower peninsular,
dramatic cliffs overlook the sea.
Home to the hardy, shaggy Welsh ponies
and on the sea coast -
you can almost taste the tantalizing
cuisine, Welsh cakes, I love most!

Cockle picking ensues and on sandy
shores the Welsh railways,
hauled coal from Rhonda valley, in bygone days.

Home of tough game rugby, and Welsh anthem
"Bread of heaven".

Welsh costume delights - it's then, I
know I've crossed the Severn.

Shadows move across Pen-y-Fan, Brecon
Beacons, a magical place.
Mountain rescue teams await,
to emergencies they race.
The red Welsh dragon roars,
its claw poised in mid-air!
Wales - land of myth and legend, the
Welsh folk love to share!

Never will I forget this land, of blue-
grey sea and green hills,
forever in my heart, it will always thrill,
it will...

Laura Sanders

* Welcome to Wales

 Laura lives in the beautiful
countryside of Dorset, not far from
the town of Shaftesbury, famed for
its historic Abbey and Gold hill.
She draws inspiration from walks
and visits to local areas of interest,
observing nature and the various passing of the
seasons. She loves writing poetry, particularly
rhyming poetry and has dealt with a wide variety
of subjects. Her other passion is music and she

plays numerous musical instruments, including the ukulele and classical and acoustic guitar. She has composed many songs and has enjoyed being in the Shaftesbury ukulele band.

SHORT STORIES

CYNEFIN

by Linda Pook

USING her stick to pivot herself forward, she struggled up the mountain track. There was a time when she would have skipped up here with her face to the mountain and the light. Now her eyes stayed on the ground searching for the stone that would trip her up and make her stumble. The air was cool but not cold. Autumn was here but summer had not yet relinquished all its hold. She stopped and stretched her back, breathing deeply as she did so. She looked ahead. Nearly there and then she would rest.

Sitting on the boulder she surveyed the valley below. Dry stone walls marked her land; flowing down the sides of the valley like dark rivers. White dots wandered across the grass. Her sheep. A few more weeks and she would need to move them in. And that would be the last time. They were all off to the autumn market in town. She wouldn't get a lot for them. She was hoping they would be sold as a flock but there were no guarantees.

How would they fair in their new home? This flock she had bred for the last sixty years and her father before her. They knew no other hillside.

The Welsh language had a name for it — Cynefin. In English it translates merely as 'Habitat' or somewhere familiar but it was far more than that. Their ancestors had been born and bred in this valley; they knew no other. It was in their blood; in their DNA. Their soul; their very being breathed in the essence that was this valley.

Her eye was caught by movement around her farm buildings. The estate agent showing prospective buyers around her farm; her home. That was why she was here. She couldn't be there listening to her home, her life's work, being listed in clichés. She knew the farm was outdated but she remembered it when all was serviceable and sometimes even new. The first time they'd had a fridge rather than the marble in the pantry. Its home was under the stairs and there it hummed throughout her childhood. Then came the large fridge/freezer, too tall for under the stairs so her grandmother's dresser was pushed into the corner in the kitchen to make room for this modern beast.

The kitchen table, scarred and worn through life times of use. It sat eight, with plenty of elbow room but she had known it crammed with the farm workers. Their solid bodies squeezed around it. Little by little the farm hands were no longer needed and the guests at the table drifted to one end. Now there was only her; an island in the vastness of the table. Her mealtimes silent where there had once been loud chatter, banter and guffaws of laughter.

Would the new owners keep the kitchen range?

She understood they were all the fashion once again. She had kept it, in or out of fashion. She gave a small smile. She'd bet that the range would never again hold small lambs in its warming cupboard nor the rag rug ease her knees as she fed them from the bottles. Two o'clock feeds with the chill at her back as she knelt to them; eyes bleary and hands unsteady with tiredness.

No! She couldn't be doing that anymore. Now she was headed for a modern little house in the village; only a few miles away but it could be a universe away. It was still in the valley but not her part of it. Not her accustomed place; her cynefin. The young girl had exulted its modern comforts; central heating and on a timer. No more fires to bank, to sweep to set. A clean white bathroom with hot water on demand. Not an immersion heater and a half hour wait before a quick strip in a chilly room. This, indeed, would be luxury but what of her garden? Her vegetable plot? The orchard next to the chicken coops? Would she still know the seasons if she was not out in her valley watching for the signs? How would she know the time if she didn't watch the finger of early sunlight travel across the far wall of her bedroom?

She sighed heavily. The air not relieving the tightness in her chest. She knew this was grief. Grieving that she was no longer that carefree girl who had scampered up to this rocky crag. Nor the young woman who had told her secrets to the wind and sky knowing they would be kept. Not even the matron who had come here to sob at the hardness of life before going back dry eyed and resolute. Now she was an old woman who had come to admit that she could no longer care for her sheep, her farm, her valley.

Her valley. Her eyes roamed again the skyline, the folds and rocks of her land. She knew every dip and hollow; every stream and runnel. There was not a patch of the valley she had not walked many times over. This was her valley. Its stones were in her bones; its waters in her blood. Her soul was bound to this valley Cynefin.

Belonging.

A FELLING

inspired by the recent tree felling for the HS2 project

by Linda Pook

I CAN clearly remember my awakening. The warmth of the sun on my bark, my limbs reaching up to the blue overhead and the breeze whispering around my crown. I drank in the air, the light, the water. Below ground my roots were warm and I could hear the thoughts of the older trees, welcoming me to the world.

The light winds played amongst my boughs and tickled my leaves. My sap hurried through my veins: water and nutriments to my leaves, sunlight energy to my roots. I grew strong.

One day a vibration pulsed through my roots and up into my crown but with it came a sense of urgency as the breeze whispered, "The men are coming!" What did the men want? Were we in danger? And then I espied them walking amongst our trunks. Tapping our barks, shaking their crowns. One came to me. He tapped my trunk several times and called to the others. More came and stood around me. Nodding and making sounds, it was a burble like water lapping at my roots.

Then came the terror. Two men began to swing something at my base. Each swing ended in a bite. The reverberations travelled along my body. My wound bled. Bite after bite and I began to feel my trunk tilt. I was going to fall. Then I was falling.

Limbs crashing and breaking as I collapsed to the forest floor. They had downed me: these little creatures with their biting tools had toppled my greatness. I lay stunned.

What would they do now?

They left me!

In the quiet that returned with the going of the men I could hear the chattering of the squirrel whose store of acorns, stored in my crevices, were now spilled across the

forest floor. The birds who had begun to nest tweeted their despair at all their work lost. The beetles and the ear worms, spiders and centipedes began to travel my surface. Murmurs of sorrow at my fall.

"They will take you away," one spider whispered. "I have seen this before."

Cries of despair came from the many crevices in my skin, "We will be homeless. What shall we do?"

I tried to sooth their fears, "Hush. There is time now to move. Other trees will welcome your hard work."

With squeaks and rustlings a steady procession of inhabitants began their journey to another home.

Throughout the dusk they travelled.

I could feel the emptiness when they had left.

Without my roots I could no longer hear my neighbours and so I let my mind wander.

The dew washed my skin one last time and soothed my empty crevices. The owl hooted farewell as she flitted through the trees above me. The mice scampered and skittered across my skin, disturbed by this new obstacle on their nightly trail. Even that lone predator, the fox, brought her cubs to wish me well.

My memories flowed through my waning sap. How varied time is. I had learned that all of us measure time according to our own lives. The turning of the day is but a

blink for me and mine but for the butterfly it is a lifetime. How many generations of squirrel have I seen? How many of the deer? The rabbits? Even those strange things

called men?

I remember my first sighting of men. They softly stepped through the trees, barely rustling the leaf waste on the floor; their bodies melding and sliding through the speckled sun rays. Their faces were as brown as the earth itself and if I had not felt their otherness I may have thought that they were of the tree world. I remember the arrival of my sapling man. It was a cool evening in spring when I heard it. Breathing grief and leaking water from its crown. Its leaves showed sign of wear and mud spattered them. Where were his mother trees? I knew enough about men to know that their saplings did not come into the forest on their own. Wearily this sapling climbed into a hollow made by my roots. I could feel its sorrow but now its strength was ebbing away with the cold as the dark began to settle.

I did not know whether man saplings could survive a night in the forests. I communed with the squirrels already awake and spring-cleaning their dray. Would they gather the moss and dry leaves from the winter and cover the sapling? The squirrels conferred together. They are not friends of the men: too often their kind are killed and devoured by them. However, my soft persuasion of the warmth of their dray within my trunk persuaded them.

Much of the warmth from the early sun I had stored in my leaves but now I pulled it through to those roots cradling the man sapling. It would not be a lot but it might keep the sharpness of the cold away. The sapling grieved even in its sleep and I began a soft hum as my veins did their work. All night I held the sapling, whispering of the goodness of the sun and the warmth.

The morning light crept through the forest and with it came the sound of men. They were not trying to be quiet, instead their noises echoed around us. Were these men looking for their sapling? I could feel the tread of men and then they were against my trunk and had spotted the sapling. Noises of joy now came from the men and the sapling awoke. Its grief was gone and now one of the men cradled it in its branches. I have seen much and lived long but now these small creatures called men have felled me. Why do men partake of such destruction? When they have felled the last tree will they then realise the work we do for them and the earth?

 "During lockdown I was able to devote time to a guilty pleasure — writing. My writing had previously been undertaken secretly and in snatched moments. As a former English teacher I have always been an avid reader and a lover of words for their sound and their meaning, both of which impact on my writing," says Linda. "I joined the Bedwas Writers' Circle and, with their encouragement, I began to seriously focus on my writing and on sharing it with others. These stories are as much due to the members encouragement as my enthusiasm. I am a recently joined member of the Bedwas Writers' Circle and was given your details for a submission."

UNDER THE LONG HILL

by Alan Hawley

O NCE, high up under the drovers' road, under the unfenced sheepland of the Long Hill, there stood the house and yard, barns and cottages of a farm. In fact it stands there still, not greatly changed, if you care to go and look.

The lady of the house was young and pretty. She was the wife of the farmer, and they were in love. The farmer was a kind, gentle man; a man willing to work hard so that his wife should want for nothing, and that the land should come to their heirs in at least as good heart as it came to him.

Her husband's shepherds lived in the farm cottages; their wives were her housemaid and cook. In the meadow a fat Welsh cob cropped the grass, her foal at foot; in the yard a sheepdog barked, ignored by a cat on a windowsill. From her windows the lady looked out over the seasons and half the world. They prospered, the seasons passed, and the lady bore a dark-haired son.

One day, as the lady crossed her yard, a fair-haired traveller chanced to pass on the drovers' road. Recklessly, he whistled and beckoned. Wondering at herself, she went out to him, and they walked briefly together on the hill and briefly lay together. He had no Welsh, and only uncouth nouns of English. In any case, they spoke little. He was neither kind nor gentle. In half an hour he was whistling on his way. Two months later he passed again, called out again, and again the lady left her son in his cradle and went out onto the hill.

Over the following months and years she looked out for the fair-haired traveller on the drovers' road, hoping that he would come once more, and hoping that he would not. If he passed the house a third time, she did not know it. The lady bore a second son, who grew dark at first and then fair.

Their elder son was content, and more than content, to learn the work of the farm, and later to take it upon himself. Her second son grew ever more restless: as soon as he thought he was old enough, and before the lady herself thought so, he left the farm. His intention was to enlist, or emigrate, or to find his proper place in life in a city. Brief, optimistic letters arrived from Shrewsbury, Chester, Liverpool, and then they heard no more. The lady found herself looking out again for a fair-haired man on the road above the house, but this time the traveller was not anonymous. As the years passed, two faces merged in her mind and shared the name of her second son.

With the coming of the camera to this border country, we have a portrait of the lady. She and her husband sit on new mahogany dining chairs, which have been brought out of doors and set in front of the house. He is in his best suit; she wears a grand, rather austere dress trimmed with lace. It looks black in the photograph but it is in fact dark green. Behind them stand their son and his beautiful wife and at their knees stand their two beautiful granddaughters. Beside the family, in a line, are the farm and household staff, all in their chapel clothes. They are flanked by their children, arranged by the photographer in order of size. A black and white dog sits at the farmer's foot; a tortoiseshell cat sleeps on a sill. We cannot see the mare and foal, for they are behind the camera but we have only to follow the little girls' eyes.

Photography in those days was staged and formal, exposure times long and collars tight, so we do not expect smiles. But we cannot miss the uncontrived contentment all in the picture show. Many years later we look again at the photograph, this time over the lady's shoulder. She is a widow. Her granddaughters, children then, are now both married. She wonders at the nature of the past, which is at the same time so far away and yet so close. And that dog in the picture must be, she thinks, the mother of the dog now asleep at her feet. It does not matter but in fact one dog is the granddaughter of the other, for she has forgotten a generation. The lady's lost, fair-haired son has two half-sisters. One lives in a far distant country; the other not five miles away. When from time to time they meet, the lady finds herself drawn to this daughter of her valley neighbour. She does not know, nor wonder, why.

THE MEETING AT THE FORD

The setting is the once strategically important Rhydwhyman Ford on the river Severn, near present-day Caerhowell and just below Hen Domen, the site of Roger of Montgomery's timber castle. Hendomen was succeeded by the (stone) castle in what is now the town of Montgomery, and which was newly built when the Treaty of Montgomery was signed there in September 1267.

by Alan Hawley

THE meeting at the ford is not a straightforward matter. Ambassadors argue its etiquette at length but their debate comes down to this: how many feet are to stay dry? In the end the answer is, none. The King of England wades across to Wales (or, in his view, to more of England), where he meets the Prince of Wales (until now merely the Prince of Aberffraw and Lord of Snowdon). They greet each other guardedly but with exaggerated politeness. Both, of course, speak French. Both then wade back into what everyone, nearly, agrees to be England.

With theatrical bonhomie Henry III and Llywelyn ap Gruffydd proceed to the castle together, there to argue about, and then to sign, the Treaty of Montgomery. They leave, each on their respective sides of the ford, the short-straw-drawing contingents of their escorts, along with a pair of impractical, much bepennated pavilions, common soldiery not for the use of.

Henry is not strong enough to wrest control of Wales from Llywelyn, so he pretends he has already done so and offers to sell it back. Llywelyn believes that Henry's weakness will not last and so plays his part in the charade. The Treaty of Montgomery records the price to be paid, in instalments, for Wales; payments on which, to nobody's surprise, Llywelyn later defaults. The financial details, however, are not why the Treaty of Montgomery is important to historians. It is important to historians because on no other occasion has an English king ever recognised the right of anyone (other than himself) to exploit the Welsh.

Meanwhile, left to their own devices at the ford, the two batches of common soldiery posture and jeer across the river for as long as their own etiquette requires, then compare and then pool their rations and rosters. Their task is made simple because both sets of officers are on the same, fire-and-kitchen side of the river and the warning of the approach of an officer is language-independent: tone of voice is sufficient.

The soldiers find their duty, which is to guard

the ford, an easy one, because the only people who want to cross it are bumpkins: simple, guileless, open-faced rustics, unarmed, unless you count the horrible-looking horns on the hairy cattle which they never seem to be without. In fact, the same small herd of biddable, bilingual cattle cross the river, backwards and forwards, many times, each time in the company of a different group of Welsh or English villagers, all of whom burn with the common defining passion of the locality, which is nosiness.

Perhaps places have memories which are more than the presence of the effects of the past; more than the things which we find if we look, or dig. If so, it is possible that the land at the ford remembers a meeting of monarchs. It may remember too, the crossing's temporary custodians (themselves equally ignorant), who ask traversing locals if they would care to know what their betters, up at the castle, are talking about. It may recall the locals' straight-faced replies: indeed; of course they would; Tipyn bach – a little bit.

Whatever treaties may say, this beautiful borderland is not for sale. It does not belong to the seller beforehand, nor to the purchaser afterwards, and it and the people who live there know this. It and they do not care who bends a gouty knee to whom. They are interested in the future: they know that what has been created there is valuable and must not be lost. They are interested in the past, remembering with gratitude those who have made this a good place to be. They are interested in the present, because it's where they live.

 Born in London E17 Alan was educated near but not at Harrow School. He survived an explosives course, that is, a chemistry degree, at Bristol University and got a stop-gap job as a civil servant, which lasted until retirement. In between, Alan got married, an Arabian horse, in that order, and then another Arabian horse and so on. They moved to Wales, to a demolishable house with nice stables and fields. "We really like it here," he says. He came across a Lifetime Learning leaflet, which mentioned creative writing. "Writing is just words, and I know plenty. Easy. Or so I thought," he says...

THE KEEPER OF CAREW CASTLE

by Kay Middlemiss

I SEE YOU. I watch you searching for me, excited and hopeful, yet scared of finding me. I hear your chatter, reading aloud from the guide book. I feel the anxiety of the tour guide who knows I am close by tonight. Will it be a shadow on the smooth, stone wall? Or a face at an empty window? Will it be a gentle touch on the shoulder or a footstep on the turret stair? I am here but you will not see me for I am hidden in another century.

"I am Princess Nest of Carew Castle in Pembrokeshire and this is my story:

Do you know what love is? Have you experienced that passion? Felt the arms of a strong man around you? If you have, then you will understand me.

In Wales, as in other places I believe princesses are born to be items of trade – married into other noble families for the benefit of their house. We are the peace offerings that end wars; we forge power between our menfolk but we are humbled. We are creatures without choice, driven by the will of the men who own our lives.

I am Nest, daughter of King Rhys ap Tewdwr, one of the four kings of Wales. I am also considered to be the most beautiful and desired of women. Twenty years before my birth, William of Normandy had conquered England but his son, King William II, was still fighting for sovereignty of that fierce and beautiful land to the west. My father was killed in battle when I was but a girl and I was taken into the care of the English king. There I became the young mistress of his brother, later to become Henry I, and bore him a son.

My family's kingdom was given to the Norman knight Gerald of Windsor and I was given in marriage to Gerald as part of the settlement. He was good to me and built Carew Castle for me. During our years together, I gave him three sons and one daughter.

However, to conquer is one thing, to hold is another. It was a time of conflict and there were constant battles between the usurping Norman lords and the noble Houses of Wales. People changed allegiances and you knew not friend from foe. My cousin Owain, the son of Cadwgon, King of Powys, came to visit and he fell in love with me. He devised a plot to storm the castle and kidnap me. I had been forewarned of the event and helped my husband to escape before I was captured by Owain's men. I was not an unwilling prisoner and during the time I spent with Owain I bore him two children.

Following reprisals, Owain fled to Ireland and I

returned to my husband Gerald and bore him one more son. It is a woman's duty to bear sons, or daughters who will be the mothers of sons.

When Gerald died in battle, I had a choice to make. A woman may not own property so, to either remarry, or to enter a convent are the only options for her. I chose the former and married Hait, the sheriff of Pembrokeshire. We had one son. On Hait's death, I married Stephen, Constable of Cardigan Castle and with him I also had a son.

It is recorded that I have born twenty children during my lifetime but records are not always accurate.

So, why am I telling you this? Because I am the one you have come to see:

I am the shadow glimpsed on a bare wall.

I am that low sigh heard in a silent room.

I am the soft fabric that touches you when no one is nearby.

I am a memory.

I am Nest, Princess of Pembrokeshire."

Following a career in the airline industry where I was fortunate to see the world, mixing with many nationalities and cultures, I moved to the beautiful Isle of Anglesey. We renovated a near-derelict converted church with a large garden, dogs, cats and flock of pigeons: inspirations for many stories. With Joy Mawby — also represented in this book — we formed Copper Writers. The group has published two anthologies of work by local writers and part-organized the first Anglesey Writing Festival. I write for pleasure not profit, enjoying competitions and writing events.

THE RECITAL

by Janice Morgan

I AM here, wherever here may be. My surroundings are alien. I no longer exist in human form. All that's left is my soul. I have no physical presence, yet I feel liberated. But do I want this freedom that has been thrust upon me? I am lost, lonely and afraid.

It started with the orchestral concert at the Wales Millennium Centre in Cardiff. The guest pianist glided on to the stage and sidled on to the stool in front of the grand piano. He awaited his cue. When it came, he raised his porcelain white hands in graceful splendour then let them drift down on to the keys. The fluid movement of his fingers unlike anything I had ever seen. I swear no bones lay hidden beneath the flesh.

The hands belonged to a slight eerie figure of a man dressed completely in black. His face, spectre white, topped with slashed-back, funeral-black hair, seemed to exist only as a power source for the hands.

There came a time during the performance when he used just one hand to play. During this time, the other hand floated in the air and swirled, the fingers a nest of snakes writhing in time to the music's charm. One of them seemed to point straight at me; the evil eye of the viper seeing all.

The pianist rose and took a bow, I saw the paleness of his face, the white hands folded across his concave stomach reminiscent of a creature that lived in the darkness of the earth's bowels, the dark clothing worn only to give it form. After polite applause I rose with the rest of the audience and left the theatre.

But I was not alone. The hands floated in front of me all the way home. No matter which way I turned my head they followed my eyes. I couldn't blame the illusion on alcohol because the only refreshment taken had been coffee, and I am not usually prone to autosuggestion.

Once home I raided my drinks cabinet in search of something strong, hoping it would help to banish the image from my mind. I swallowed a large cognac and retired to bed. The image continued to taunt me, my bed turned into a tumble drier, the bedclothes twisting and turning around me as I got hotter and hotter. Eventually exhaustion took over and I slept.

I awoke with a feeling of terror, sensing the presence of the hands again. They drifted slowly downward from the ceiling as if towards an imaginary keyboard. The fingers writhed and tapped, first in gentle waves creating a haunting melody, and then they grew stronger and firmer as the music grew more tempestuous. They flew along the virtual piano keys, faster and faster, harder, and more intense. Finally, they rose upward. Like claws they hovered as if in readiness to play the final chords.

Instead of pouncing on to the invisible keyboard they pounced towards my grave-cold body. Corpse-stiff with fear, I was unable to move. They formed a stranglehold around my neck, and I knew no more...until now.

I am here, wherever here may be...

 Janice Morgan writes short stories and poetry but has also written a psychological thriller and a children's book. For most of her working life she worked as a bookkeeper/cashier but retrained as a teacher, completing a Cert Ed with distinction, and a first-class honours degree in Education and Training, as a mature student. It was during this time that she became interested in psychology and this has influenced her written words. Her psychological thriller, Borderline, has been well received.

THE PRESENT

by Joy Mawby

"**D**AD," I say, "Can I have a bucket and spade please?"

"Aren't you too old for sandcastles now you're eight?" dad teases.

"I'll never be too old for sandcastles."

While we are in the shop, I see a little weather house. A lady, in yellow painted clothes is standing outside one door. A man, in blue, is standing just inside another.

"The lady goes in and the man comes out when it's going to rain," explains the shop-lady.

I love the little house and have an idea. "Can I buy it as a present for mum?" I ask dad. "I've got enough pocket money."

Dad nods.

On Benllech beach, dad takes a photo of me. I've made a castle and it's going to be knocked down by the waves because the tide's coming in. I'm dancing away from the waves. I love dancing. I want to be a dancer when I grow up — like my mum. Madame Julianna says I'm coming on nicely.

"I wish mum was here, with us on Anglesey. I wish we were all staying at auntie Jane's and uncle

Tony's."

"I know, darling, so do I. We'll send mum this photo. She'll be happy to see we're having such a good time."

"When will she be better?"

"I don't know, Maisie. I don't know."

But he does know. I can tell he knows and he won't say it. He won't say, "Never."

His mobile rings and he walks away to answer it. I pretend to dig but really, I'm watching him. I see his face go serious. After a few minutes he returns.

"Maisie, I'll have to leave you here, with auntie and uncle for a day or two."

"Where are you going?"

"I need to go and see mum."

"Can I come?"

"Not this time, darling. I'm sure you'll do something exciting here while I'm away. I'll be back as soon as I can."

I feel tears in my eyes but I wipe them away when dad's not looking. He seems so worried. I know I must try to be brave. I quickly fetch the weather house and push it into his hand as he hurries to the car.

After auntie Jane and I have waved dad off, I do have a little cry but my auntie puts her arm round me and leads me up the side of her house to the back garden. On the patio, I see two little rolled-up tents, three sleeping bags and a box with a kettle, a frying pan and some tin plates and cups in it. I forget about mum and dad for a moment when auntie Jane says, "I thought we could make a camp in the garden, Maisie. We can have a campfire and cook sausages and beans. Will you help me put the tents up, please, so we'll have everything ready by the time uncle Tony gets home? There's nothing we like more than a night's camping."

I feel light and happy inside as we put up the tents near the bottom of the garden. We gather sticks from the little wood by the house, ready for the campfire. We've just finished when uncle Tony arrives home.

"Brilliant," he says, when I tell him auntie's idea. "I'll change into some camping gear while you start cooking."

I'm allowed to light the fire and I help cook the sausages, too. They only get a bit burnt. Auntie Jane stirs the baked beans. Uncle Tony comes outside with cups of cocoa for us all and we sit on blankets round the fire and have a feast. It's the best food I've ever tasted.

Afterwards we sing songs by the fire and play hide-and-seek. I hide under a pile of sacks in the shed and auntie and uncle can't find me for ages. After that, it's bedtime but I don't even have to wash — just brush my teeth and snuggle down in my sleeping bag. I can see stars through a gap at one end of my tent and I'm very sleepy.

It's light when auntie Jane calls my name. "Dad's on the phone," she says. She passes me her mobile.

"Maisie, I've got some news."

I feel my heart thump hard. "Is mum all right?"

"Yes, she is, darling. She has been given the most wonderful present.

"Is it better than my weather house?"

"That's fantastic, of course but this is an even better present."

I feel cross. "What have they given her, then?"

"They have given her a kidney, Maisie, a new kidney."

 Joy Mawby lives on the Isle of Anglesey in North Wales. She runs a local writing group and was involved in the production of two anthologies of work, by Anglesey writers and in organising the first Writing Festival to be held on the island. She has written and published, three memoirs of other peoples' lives and her own memoir – although this is specially for her grandchildren! Two of her plays have been staged locally and she also writes short stories and poetry.

A BROTHER'S NUDGE

by Angie Gliddon

I HADN'T been back to Pommie-land for years but decided I should go to visit relatives I hadn't seen for decades. I had enjoyed a relaxing time with my brother Sam and his wife in Cambridge but was looking forward to visiting my sister June on Anglesey, walking the coastal footpath and seeing historic sites.

"June's so lucky," said Sam, "her Jack is so devoted to her – goes well beyond the call of duty; caring for her as her arthritis gets worse. Sadly, we haven't been there for years as I no longer drive. Do give her our love."

I decided to rent a car for the journey, to give me the freedom of stopping to see English rivers and canals and the mountains of Wales. I arrived in Rhosneigr and was delighted to see the view of the sea and bay from June's window.

June was sitting in the armchair all the afternoon, while I was telling them what I'd seen that day. I was sorry to note she seemed saddened by my descriptions.

"Would you like to show me around Rhosneigr this evening?" I asked.

June burst into tears.

"There, there, dear," said Jack. "Your brother doesn't realise your condition. June really isn't fit enough to climb into a wheelchair and if she were, I couldn't push her."

"Well," I replied, "I am here now and I'll help. Would you like me to help, June?"

She looked at me tearfully. "Oh, I don't know, Andrew. I am very stiff. Last week when I tried to get into the car to go for a run in the country, we couldn't manage it."

I was horrified by this. My Ozzie friend, Mike, worked as a physio and was always telling me that exercise was crucial to maintain the ability to move for people with arthritis. I decided to think more, overnight, about whether I should try to talk to June, or to approach Jack first, in order to foster a change of attitude.

After breakfast Jack was doing the washing up – I'll say that for him, he didn't mind doing the housework, so I sat with June.

"You know, there will be some flat walks in town along the esplanade and user-friendly tracks in the country. Wouldn't you like to try and see these for yourself?"

I saw a sparkle in her eye as she replied, "Oh yes, Andrew, I'd love to. I don't mind if I look awkward or old. It's so difficult for Jack, though. He acts almost as though he's ashamed of me. He keeps me wrapped in cotton-wool and doesn't want to go outside with me."

So, the problem was with Jack. I'd have to take this carefully.

The next morning a hairdresser came to do June's hair, so I talked to Jack. I told him about my friend, Mike, and his work with patients "... and he says that it is very important for them to keep on using their muscles. If they do, they get fitter and are able to do more and more. Don't you think that June should try some special exercises? She could improve her mobility a lot."

"But this is my wife, June, who was so beautiful and fashionable. I worshipped her – I still do and I try to protect her from the prejudices of people outside. I will always love her as she is."

"But, Jack, have you ever asked her what she really wants?"

Jack shuddered and held his head in his hands. Then he looked up at me. "She never said... she always let me fuss around her and do everything..."

"Perhaps because you always made the decisions," I suggested.

At that moment the hairdresser popped her head around the door to say goodbye.

"June seems a little unsettled today," she confided. "Is everything all right?"

"I'll go and have a word with her," said Jack.

I helped the hairdresser carry her bags to her car and stayed outside for a while, enjoying the fresh sea air and the view and hoping the pair of them would come to a happy arrangement.

Eventually Jack came outside.

"Do come in, Andrew, please. June would like to ask you some questions and I think I should listen, too."

With a sense of relief, I stepped into the house, hoping that I could go out later and buy a bottle of wine for us all to celebrate.

THE TAPESTRY OF LIFE

by Angie Gliddon

WHEN I was a student at Bangor my third-year project was carried out in a home for older people. It was open to me what I did there, so I decided to play the role of a volunteer carer and write an academic report about people's interactions. That was how I met Nansi Huws.

I saw her sitting there, bending over the work she was stitching. Her fingers were bent and stiffened by arthritis; she must have found it difficult to do such fine work. Fascinated, I sat down opposite her and watched. She selected some dark grey thread and, using quite long stitches, she covered an area on the top left of the canvas. "Perhaps that's a rocky area," I thought. Then she used fine black thread and made much daintier stitches in between the grey.

I couldn't contain myself. "Hello, Mrs Huws," I said. "I'm a new visitor here and I've been watching you do your embroidery. It's fascinating. Can you show me what you're doing?"

She blinked up at me, as though it wasn't easy to adjust her vision to focus on something as far away as I was, perhaps six feet away. "Oh, I don't mind," she said. "I grew up in Bethesda, you see, from a family of quarrymen. My grandfather used to take me on walks up the Ogwen valley and I was always impressed by the great piles of slate waste on the hills around us."

"They must have been very forbidding," said I, thinking of grey stones under a grey sky on a rainy day.

"Ah," said she. "That's because you don't know them. The sun glints off the smooth surfaces so they look like jewels. That's what I'm trying to show here. Come closer to have a look."

I walked round and she indicated a chair next to hers so I sat down. She sewed another tiny black stitch but left her needle fixed in the material and passed the frame over to me.

"It's astonishing," I gasped. "It's beautiful; somehow it looks three-dimensional."

Mrs Huws looked pleased. "Good," she said, "but the tapestry isn't going to be all grey rocks. There'll be a large green field sweeping down across the picture to the little road I have started over here. I'll add a small Welsh cottage on the road with my granddaughter looking across towards the slate. I only hope I can keep on stitching 'til I finish it. I want to give it to my son for Christmas."

"That will be a wonderful present, Mrs Huws. Does your son's family still live in the valley?"

"No, sadly, they had to move after my daughter-in-law died in a road accident. He now lives near his sister so she can help look after little Megan. That's why it is so important that I make this reminder for them."

"Oh, I'm sure you are right Mrs Huws. Thanks for talking to me. Can I come and see you again next week?"

"Of course, I'd like that. Some people think I'm an old misery because I prefer sewing to playing bingo!"

I returned the next week and saw the tapestry had progressed, showing the little cottage and the varying shades of green in the valley.

"Only the pale blue sky and clouds to do now," said she.

The following week, when I went to check in, I was met by the manager of the home.

"I'm very sorry to have to tell you that Mrs Huws has passed away," she said.

"Oh dear, I'm so sorry," said I, shaken. "Please can you tell me the arrangements for her funeral? And – ah yes, her tapestry; was she able to finish it? It seemed so important to her."

"I'm afraid not, we wrapped it up and gave it to her family, with her other possessions."

I met Mrs Huws' family at the funeral and talked about the tapestry but they did not seem very interested.

"Could I see it?" I asked. And that is how this marvellous piece of art and history came into my possession. I thought about completing the work, as she had told me her intentions but I'm no great needlewoman. I decided to leave a white sky as an emblem of hope.

I still have the contact for the Huws family and one day, when Megan is older, I'll offer it to her and hope to have a chance to tell her the story behind it.

Angie Gliddon is a member of Copper Writers.

THE RELUCTANT COWBOY

by Edwina Jones

I KNEW I was dead as I was slowly being drawn to the light. I opened my eyes reluctantly. I was being observed by a puzzled-looking African-American native, dressed in traditional clothes. Did God do fancy dress? And why was he puzzled, wasn't he expecting me?

"How!" he said, holding up his hand. I knew exactly how and started to explain but a gunshot cut me short. Wasn't I dead enough? God was also startled and in one fluid movement he jumped on his horse and rode swiftly off, chased by further gunshots. I lay there terrified and realised that I was wet. Had I crossed the Styx and was I in the other place?

Then Doris Day came up to me, "Howdy mister, you're OK now. I got rid of that pesky redskin. Did he take your things?"

I started to explain, "I was at the NEC at the Dr Who convention, they make it in Wales you see, and I'm Welsh and a big fan, so..."

"What are you rambling about? You must surely have had a bump on your head. Let's get you back to the ranch." And then this slip of a girl lifted me up and put me in the back of an open wagon.

"Thank you Doris," I replied gingerly feeling bruises all over my body.

"Doris? I'm not Doris!"

"Of course you're not. It's Calamity isn't it. How on earth I've wandered onto your set I don't know."

When we arrived at the ranch, Calamity yelled, "Mom, grandma, come see what I found by the creek. I opened my mouth to speak but my legs buckled beneath me. The women picked me up as if I were a child, laying me on a day bed on the stoop. They gave me water, which I drank thirstily and it revived me enough to be able to ask them to get in touch with the paramedics as I knew all film sets had to have first aiders available - before I drifted off to sleep.

It was almost dark when I woke and the stoop seemed to be full of people, staring at me. There was pappy and grandma, pop and Mary-Kate, Calamity (actually named Tilly), Donny-Joe and Pete. I told them how I'd arrived at their film set and apologised profusely, hoping I hadn't disrupted filming too much. I explained that I'm a scriptwriter and while I was at the Dr Who convention I got into the Tardis. The door shut behind me and the lock slipped. I must have leaned against something because next thing the Tardis took off, must have hit some turbulence causing me to fall out and I ended up here, all bruised and with no sign of the Tardis, which must have developed another fault and gone off again. My ribs were aching so I asked if they had been able to get me a doctor.

"Doc Martin is a day's ride away so there's no chance he'll come and see you."

"Oh I know Martin Clunes, is he on set anywhere? Strange location for Cornwall though."

It took a long time for my situation to sink in. This was no film set and my life would never be the same again. These kind people took me in and looked after me, putting up with my strange ways and making allowances for my lack of basic skills in the cowboy department.

A year later Tilly became my wife and I became the editor of the Tumbleweed Times. We had a daughter who I insisted was named Kylie Minogue Watson as a nod to my teenage crush. Apart from local news I filled the paper with stories - my version of The Importance of Being Earnest, Of Mice and Men, To Kill a Mocking Bird and many others. A plagiarist? Me? I'm writing these stories in 1850 and folks taking the Oregon Trail pick up my newspaper as they pass through Tumbleweed Creek and spread my stories far and wide. Who knows where Wilde, Steinbeck and Lee found their inspiration? Their future is my past.

Edwina lives on Ynys Môn and is Welsh-speaking but she mainly writes in English. She has just finished her first novel and also writes short stories and poetry. She belongs to two writing groups. She was secretary for the Môntage committee which produced two anthologies of work from local authors and was also involved in organising a writing festival on the island.

Printed in Great Britain
by Amazon